I Am Wings

Poems About Love

by Ralph Fletcher
photographs by Joe Baker

Bradbury Press   New York
Maxwell Macmillan Canada Toronto
Maxwell Macmillan International
New York Oxford Singapore Sydney

Bradbury Press
Macmillan Publishing Company
866 Third Avenue
New York, NY 10022

Maxwell Macmillan Canada, Inc.
1200 Eglinton Avenue East
Suite 200
Don Mills, Ontario M3C 3N1

Macmillan Publishing Company is part of the Maxwell Communication
Group of Companies.

The text of this book is set in 13 point Optima.
Book design by Julie Y. Quan
First edition
10 9 8 7 6 5 4 3 2 1
Library of Congress Catalog Card Number 93-40259
ISBN 0-02-735395-8

To my love, JoAnn

Contents

Falling In

Falling Out

Falling In

First Look

At 8:03 A.M.
a prickle of heat
itches down my neck.

I glance up and
catch that look,
a calm, steady gaze
that holds mine fast
until I can twist away
close the metal locker
and force myself to walk
slowly
down the bursting halls

First Thought

Why would I lie?
Artie hisses
all the way to PE—
I'm telling you she
likes you, man, she really
likes you.

Just talk I think
undressing so fast
to play basketball
I pop a shirt button
and don't think of her
until this one play
I spin off a pick
take a bounce pass
fake once lean in
bank it neatly off glass
and for maybe a half second
she does enter
my mind

I Am Wings

We're at Rexham Beach
when you stroll by
wearing the tightest
smile
your tanned shoulders
whispering to me
whispering clear as day

"Wings! I am wings!"

floating past the spot
where I stand
nailed to the shore
one foot in ocean
one on dry land
but already way
way over my head

Crush Blush

You'd have to be blind
not to see how bad
Katie Berdolt has it
for skinny Aaron Ray
puppydogging after him
in school or out

In English class
Mike Blum yells out:
"Katie's got a CRUSH
on Aaron!"

She tries a half-shrug
but her face betrays her
slowly turning red
right down the hair roots
with everybody howling
OOOOOOOOOOO!

An amazing red color
I think the word is
crimson
I think the word is
true

The Note

I write you a note
unsigned
folded and tucked
inside the novel
you've been reading
Lord of the Flies or
Huckleberry Finn my
heart pounding so hard
I can't see straight.

Next day in homeroom
your eyes look different.

All I want to say is:
don't worry about
any hidden meanings
or crazy symbolism
like in English class.

This note means
only what it says:

Springtime
and I wish I knew you

Phone Call

In kindergarten
we played house
got married
and had 99 kids.

In first grade
you told me first
when you peed
in your pants.

Remember that summer
we glued apple seeds
onto Popsicle sticks
and tried selling them?

Now you want to go out?
To the movies?
Like on a real date?
Well, ah, um: sure.

Named

At the video store
you're in comedy
I'm deep in horror
the very first time
you speak my name:

"Hey, Lee, c'mere!"

My name in your mouth
my whole self
squeezing through
that little gap
in your front teeth

First Touch

Halfway through the movie
at the most boring part
you slowly reach up
and sort of backwards
to rub my left shoulder
and keep on rubbing it
until the movie screen
becomes a bright blur.

"Shoulder," I think
all the way home
feeling it tingle
feeling it glow:
"I have a shoulder."

Fireworks

on the grass field
sitting back to back
and spine to spine
elbows locked
laughing and leaning
backwards and forwards
your way and mine
the firecrackers
spidering crazily
exploding above us
with a CRACK
and a ba-BOOOOM
that thumps the gut
though mainly it's
your spine
against mine
and fiery
explosions
up and down
the line

The New World

In the movie dark
I explore it—
notch by knuckle by
smooth flat land:
the new world
that is your hand.

First Kiss

I'll never forget
that empty barn
smell of dry hay
those long columns
of dusty light

for one whole minute
you and I breathed
the same breath

19

Space

How you hated
the little gap,
small extra   space
between your front teeth.

"My folks wouldn't
shell out the bucks
to get it fixed."

But I wanted to say:
Leave that space.
Let it be.

Leave space
in your life
for me.

Nature

Friday nights
I come to your aunt's house
drink Coke watch cable TV
while you baby-sit the twins.

One hot night
loud thunder rolls in.
We stand at the window
arms almost touching
breathing the electric air
but the twins wake up
screaming bloody murder.
You smile, elbow me hard,
run upstairs to get them.

For almost an hour
they tremble on your lap
soothed by your warmth
and soft voice:

"Thunder won't hurt you.
Don't worry. It's okay.
It's only nature."

Justin and Frank

The first day of school
outside by the flagpole
Luke Sufchek screaming
"Fags! Stinkin' fags!"
pushes Frank down hard
so Justin jumps in
gets beat up awful bad
Mr. Root pulls him off
Sufchek gets suspended
for the tenth time and
Justin has to go home
all covered with blood

On Saturday it's hot
and we go to the beach

I walk down to the Point
find Frank and Justin
sitting together
all by themselves
Justin's lip still puffy
helping Frank put lotion
on the big lump
on his forehead

which sort of matches
the lump
in my throat

Counting Stars

On the beach
you teach me
to count stars
the first one
brave and clear
the second a
reluctant twin
now a third a fourth
until all at once
stars are everywhere
and around thirteen
we have both lost count

The first shy kiss
leads to another
then two more
back-to-back
and it doesn't
take long
before I
lose count

Winter Twilight

cones of a sumac bush
dark flames
against the cold sky

I walk with bare hands
still warm
from our last touch

Basket

we walk
holding hands
our fingers
woven together
hanging between us
like a basket
soft but strong
and snugly knit
with room enough
for love to fit

Falling Out

The Note Again

One night
after the game
you mention it—
the anonymous note
found in early March
tucked inside your book.

"Springtime
and I wish I knew you"

How it made you wonder
How it troubled your sleep

I change the subject,
a first small betrayal
beneath the star-scarred sky.

Playing with Fire

You said you
loved me
that afternoon
behind the woodpile
but when your father
collapsed at work
and died
without a hint
without a good-bye
your face
got all blurry gray
and I knew enough
to stay away.

All winter your ma
burned the wood
he had stacked
in the garage
to keep you warm
the wood so dry it
burned without smoke
until all the wood
was gone.

You said you
loved me
but when
I saw your face
I understood
we were just
playing
with that word.

First Fight

All the way home
I tried to forget
how your lip twitched
how your face flinched

I walked alone
under a huge rainbow
beautiful and damaged
upper arch worn away
just two broken pieces
dangling from the sky

Waiting for the Splash

Last night
after you hung up
I wrote you a poem
hoping it might
change your heart.

This morning
I tell myself:
Get serious, man.
Someone once compared
writing a poem
and hoping it will
change the world
to dropping rose petals
down a deep well

waiting for the splash.

Owl Pellets

A month ago
in biology lab
you sat close to me
knee touching mine
your sweet smell
almost drowning out
the formaldehyde stink
which crinkled up
your nose
while I dissected
our fetal pig.

Now I take apart
this owl pellet
small bag that holds
skin and hair and bones
little skeletons
what the owl ate
but couldn't digest
and coughed back up.

You sit with Jon Fox
ignore me completely
laugh at his dumb jokes
let your head fall onto
his bony shoulder
while I attempt
to piece together
with trembling hands
the tiny bones
of a baby snake.

Certain things
are just about
impossible
to swallow.

Faithful Elephants

The day you break up with me
Mr. Peterson reads to the class
that picture book
Faithful Elephants
about those zoo elephants
that had to be killed
in Japan
during World War Two

Too smart for poison potatoes
their hides too tough for needles
the three elephants got slowly
starved

I catch you wiping tears
and want to say

Hey, my feelings for you
are exactly like
those elephants

You think I can take
something big as that
just snap my fingers
make them
disappear?

I can't shoot them
I can't poison them
I can't see any other way
but let
        them
            starve

Ten Reasons Why

1. There's nothing wrong with your smile or breath.

2. I just can't breathe.

3. I feel like we're both underwater.

4. I miss my friends.

5. I miss my time.

6. I miss breathing my own air.

7. We're starting to become one of *those* couples.

8. We're beginning to share a personality.

9. They never mention me without mentioning you in the same sentence.

10. I want my own sentence.

Changing Channels

It was like nothing
I'd seen at the movies.

You never sat me down
with a husk in your voice.

It happened BANG: like you
just changed channels.

Your warm Wednesday eyes
went cold on Thursday morn.

Would you please explain
exactly what has changed?

Won't You Come Home Bill Bailey?

You liked vegetarian food
plus those old-time songs
that drove me up a wall

THE RAIN IN SPAIN
FALLS MAINLY ON THE PLAIN

I liked red meat (rare)
and rock music (hard)
I adored horror films
you loved books
and finally
we split up

I gave back your books
you gave back my tapes
that seemed to end it
except for one thing

I AIN'T HAD NO LOVIN' SINCE
JANUARY FEBRUARY JUNE AND JULY

your old-fashioned songs
jumbling around in my head
like sneakers in a dryer
keeping me up day and night

REMEMBER THAT RAINY EVENING
I THREW YOU OUT
WITH NOTHING BUT A
FINE-TOOTH COMB?

Please come over right away
you gotta clean out this stuff

PLEASE RELEASE ME LET ME GO
I DON'T LOVE YOU ANYMORE

I mean it: I'm going nuts

Daedalus and Icarus

We're split up
don't talk
but stuck in English
two rows apart

The mythology unit
Daedalus and Icarus
fashioned their own wings
from wax and feathers
but I keep remembering
that day at Rexham Beach
your bare tanned shoulders
whispering to me:

"Wings! I am wings!"

Icarus flew too close
to the sun and drowned

I breathe deep
keep telling myself:

this is just mythology
this has no
connection
to my life

The Truth

It's this simple:
I found you beautiful
almost beyond belief
if you want the truth
but who really wants the truth
when it comes to love?

The Tree

A Christmas tree
cut from its roots
and brought inside
for lights and tinsel
still drinks water
at least a quart a day
or it will dry up.

Cut flowers:
same thing.

Water tricks them
into thinking
they are alive.

Even though
it's over
between us
the sight of you
still tastes
like cold water
to these dead
thirsty eyes.

Lies, Lies

I never loved you:
Not once. Not once.

The "love-basket" made
when we walked
holding hands?
Fingers and thumbs
and nothing more.

This is it:
my last last note.

When I finish this
I'll run outside
through the dark
through the rain.

PS Forget what I said
about the space
in your teeth.
You really should
get that fixed.

Seeds

There's this new kid
from around Chicago
who smiled at me
this really cute smile
during lunch.

That afternoon
in late autumn
I walk a field
all dry and dead
nothing left but
seeds:
burrs and prickles
pearly bayberries
cat-o'-nine-tails.

Milkweed pods
by the thousand
cleaning the silk
from their purses.

I collect a bunch
and head home
whistling
pockets stuffed with
new beginnings.

ABOUT THE AUTHOR

As an author and consultant, Ralph Fletcher works with teachers and students across the United States. He has a degree in writing from Columbia University and is the author of two books on how to teach writing—*Walking Trees* and *What a Writer Needs* (both Heinemann). He has published two volumes of poetry, *Water Planet* and *The Magic Nest*; his poems have also appeared in many anthologies. Ralph Fletcher lives with his wife, JoAnn, and four boys in Durham, New Hampshire.